EPOSSUMONDAS

WRITTEN BY **Coleen Salley**

ILLUSTRATED BY Janet Stevens

Harcourt, Inc.

Orlando   Austin   New York   San Diego   London

Epossumondas was his mama's and his auntie's sweet little patootie. They just loved him to death.

Epossumondas used to go see his auntie most every day, and she nearly always gave him something to take home with him.

One day she gave him
a piece of rich gold cake.

Epossumondas took it in
his hand, scrunched his
hand up tight, and went
along home.

On his way home, he passed
Alligator, and Alligator asked,
"What you got, Epossumondas?"
"Cake," he replied.
"Hmm. Don't look much like cake
to me," said Alligator.

When Epossumondas got home, his mama looked at that fist full of crumbs, and she said, "Epossumondas, what do you have in your hand?"

"Cake, Mama. Auntie gave it to me."

"Oh, Epossumondas, you don't have the sense you were born with! That's no way to carry cake! The way to carry cake is to put the cake on your head, put a hat on your head, and come along home. Do you hear me, Epossumondas?"

"Yes, Mama."

By and by on another day when Epossumondas was visiting his auntie, this time she gave him a pound of freshly churned butter to take home with him.

Epossumondas put it on his head, put a hat on his head, and went along home.

On his way home, he passed Raccoon, and Raccoon asked, "What you got, Epossumondas?"

"Butter," he replied.

"Hmm. Don't look much like butter to me," said Raccoon.

When Epossumondas got home, his mama looked at him, and she said, "Epossumondas, what do you have in that hat?"

"Butter, Mama. Auntie gave it to me."

"Oh, Epossumondas, you don't have the sense you were born with! That's no way to carry butter! The way to carry butter is to wrap it up in some leaves and carry it down to the brook, and you cool it in the water, and you cool it in the water, and you cool it in the water, and then you take it up carefully in your hands and come along home. Do you hear me, Epossumondas?"

"Yes, Mama."

By and by on another day when Epossumondas was visiting his auntie, this time she gave him a sweet little puppy dog to take home with him.

So Epossumondas wrapped it up in some leaves and carried it down to the brook.

And he cooled it in the water, and he cooled it in the water, and he cooled it in the water, and then he took it up carefully in his hands and went along home.

On his way home, he passed Nutria, and Nutria asked, "What you got, Epossumondas?"

"A puppy," he replied.

"Hmm. Don't look much like a puppy to me," said Nutria.

When Epossumondas got home, his mama looked at that poor little bedraggled puppy, and she said, "Epossumondas! What do you have in your hands?"

"A puppy, Mama. Auntie gave it to me."

"Oh, Epossumondas! Epossumondas! You don't have the sense you were born with! That's no way to carry a puppy! The way to carry a puppy is to put the puppy on the ground, tie a piece of string around the puppy dog's neck, and take the piece of string and come along home. Do you hear me, Epossumondas?"

"Yes, Mama."

Well, by and by on another day when Epossumondas was visiting his auntie, this time she gave him a freshly baked loaf of bread to take home with him.

Epossumondas put the bread on the ground, tied a piece of string around it, took the other end of the string, and went along home.

On his way home, he passed Armadillo, and
Armadillo asked, "What you got, Epossumondas?"
"Bread," he replied.
"Hmm. Don't look much like bread to me," said
Armadillo.

When Epossumondas got home, his mama looked at the THING on the end of the string, and she said, "Epossumondas! What do you have on the end of that string?"

"Bread, Mama. Auntie gave it to me."

"Ooooooh! Epossumondas! Epossumondas! You DON'T have the sense you were born with! You never DID have the sense you were born with! You never WILL have the sense you were born with! Now I'm not telling you any more ways of bringing truck home, and I don't want you going to see your auntie, either. I'll go see her myself."

And Epossumondas's mama got her basket, but before she left, she said, "Epossumondas, do you see those six pies cooling there on the porch?"
"Yes, Mama."

"Well, Epossumondas, you be careful about stepping on those pies!"
Then Mama went off to see Auntie.

And then—Epossumondas WAS careful about stepping on those pies. He stepped right in the MIDDLE of EVERY one!

STORYTELLER'S NOTE

Long before authors, books, and publishers existed, storytellers wove folktales that enthralled groups of adults—and any children who might be listening In those days, storytelling was not limited to an audience of children, as is prevalent in modern times. The oral tradition was a way of communicating with an entire community.

Folktales have endured for many centuries because they entertain, stretch the imagination, evoke emotion, nurture a sense of humor, and pique curiosity about other cultures. They have attempted to explain nature, natural phenomena, and even the behavior of animals and humans. Similar tales appear again and again throughout the world, reinforcing the truth that people everywhere are more alike than different. And all of these ideas and themes are delivered in packages filled with action, heroes and heroines, lessons, and satisfying endings—all the elements of a good story.

EPOSSUMONDAS is a type of tale called a noodlehead story. Mishaps occur but are not caused deliberately. The humor is gentle and silly. The plot may be highly improbable, but not impossible—it COULD happen. Some outstanding noodlehead stories are about the wise Nasreddin Hodja (Turkish), those amiable Fools of Chelm (Jewish), lazy Heinz (German), foolish Jack (British), Jean Sot (Cajun), and Epaminondas (southern United States).

Throughout the ages, storytellers have embellished, adapted, deleted, and added to the tales they tell. The details change, but the heart of the story remains. We recognize old favorites in a new rendition. Thus EPOSSUMONDAS—a new name for a classic character—has moved from the human world into the world of animals. And if you think that little possum is just foolish, look closer. Maybe he's full of mischief, trying to get a rise out of his mama so he can escape all those errands! Does he remind you of anyone you know?

—COLEEN SALLEY

For information about permission to reproduce selections from this book,
please write Permissions, Houghton Mifflin Harcourt Publishing Company,
215 Park Avenue South, NY, NY 10003.

www.hmhbooks.com

Library of Congress Cataloging-in-Publication Data
Salley, Coleen.
Epossumondas/Coleen Salley; illustrated by Janet Stevens.
p.   cm.
Summary: A retelling of a classic tale in which a well-intentioned young
possum continually takes his mother's instructions much too literally.
[1. Fools and jesters—Folklore.   2. Folklore.]
I. Stevens, Janet, ill.   II. Title.
PZ8.1.S2168Ep   2002
398.21—dc21   2001004906
ISBN 978-0-15-216748-6

SCP 10 9 8 7 6 5 4
4500446195

Printed in China

The illustrations in this book were done in watercolor, colored pencil,
and photographic and digital elements on watercolor paper.
The display type was set in Spumoni.
The text type was set in Big Dog
Color separations by Bright Arts Ltd., Hong Kong
Printed and bound by RR Donnelley, China
Production supervision by Sandra Grebenar and Ginger Boyer
Designed by Lydia D'moch

For my children:
George, Genevieve, and David,
who have always been
my biggest fans. I love you!
—C. S.

For Coleen,
my favorite character
—J. S.

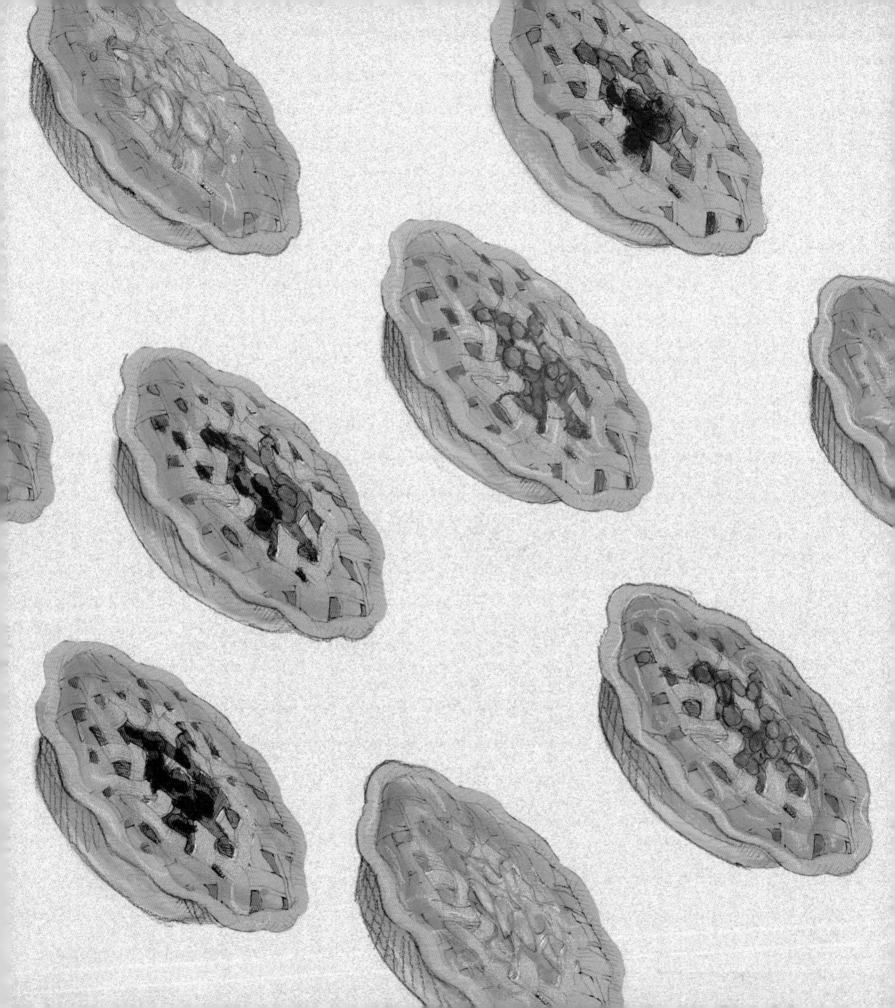